SPIDER McDREW AND THE EGYPTIANS

Written by Alan Durant

Illustrated by Philip Hopman

 Collins

CHAPTER 1

Spider McDrew was a hopeless case. Everyone said so –
his mum, the teachers at Parkfield School, the other
children in his class. They said it when they looked at
him with his sprouty hair like the leaves of a spider plant
(that's why his nickname was Spider). They said it when
he had clothes on all inside out and back to front ...
and they said it when he got things wrong. He got things
wrong a lot because he tended to carry on thinking
about something after everyone else had stopped, so he
was often one step behind.

Spider's class was learning about the Romans. They had looked at books about Romans and coloured in maps of the Roman Empire. Soon they were going to dress up in Roman costumes and do a school assembly. To prepare for it, their teacher, Mr Smithers, was taking them on a day trip to the museum.

"Has anyone been before?" he asked the class. A few children put up their hands.

"Please sir, I went to see the mummies, sir," Darren Kelly said breathlessly. "They was wicked."

"*Were* wicked, Darren," Mr Smithers corrected him.

"Yes, sir, they was," Darren confirmed.

"Mummies had their brains pulled out through their noses," Neil Phillips added happily.

"Ugh, yuk!" exclaimed Hannah Stewart.

"Thank you, Neil, I don't think we want to hear any more about that," said Mr Smithers.

Spider McDrew put up his hand.

"Yes, Spider?" said Mr Smithers.

Spider smiled. "I've got a mummy," he said.

At once, the class erupted into loud laughter.

"Spider's got a mummy!" cried Kip Keen.

"We've all got a mummy," groaned Jason Best.

"You're mad, Spider," Darren Kelly remarked.

Mr Smithers clapped his hands and called for quiet.
"Now, let's hear no more about mummies," he said
sternly. "It's Roman things, not Egyptian, that we're
going to look at."

Spider stared down at his desk, feeling stupid.

He'd meant to say that he had a model of an Egyptian
mummy at home – his mum had given it to him for
his last birthday – but, as usual, the words had come
out wrong.

 # CHAPTER 2

The next day on the coach everyone was very excited –
even Spider. He was sitting next to his best friend,
Jack Smith.

"I can't wait to see the mummies," Spider said.
He'd been thinking about mummies ever since the
previous day.

"What mummies?" Jack Smith asked.

"The Egyptian mummies," said Spider.

"Spider, we're not going to look at the mummies," Jack
Smith laughed. "Mr Smithers said we're going to look
at Roman things – like coins and stuff."

"Oh," said Spider, disappointed. Coins didn't sound
nearly as interesting as mummies.

When they got to the museum, Mr Smithers handed out some sheets of paper with questions for the children to answer. Mrs Russell, the school music teacher, was helping Mr Smithers look after the children. She gave them all a pencil to write with.

"Now," said Mr Smithers, "before we start our visit, who can tell me something about the Romans?" Hannah Stewart put up her hand.
"Yes, Hannah?" said Mr Smithers.

"They were ancient, sir," Hannah declared with a smug smile.
"They liked fighting battles and conquering people," said Kip Keen.
"They were gladiators," said Jason Best. Then he and Kip had a sword fight with their pencils.

"That will do, you two," said Mr Smithers. "This is a museum, not a battlefield." He waited for Jason and Kip to stop fighting. "Now, who can tell me anything else about the Romans?" he asked. Emma Flowers put up her hand. "The Romans built Hadrian's Wall," she said.

"Very good, Emma," said Mr Smithers.

Darren Kelly waved his hand in the air. "No they never, sir!" he exploded. "My dad done it – and I helped him. You can ask my uncle."
"Your uncle?" Mr Smithers asked, puzzled.

"Yes sir," said Darren Kelly.
"My uncle's Adrian and it was his wall we built."

Mr Smithers shook his head and sighed. "I think Emma was talking about *Hadrian*, not Adrian, Darren," he said. "Hadrian was a Roman Emperor."

Mrs Russell joined in. "What else did the Romans build?" she asked.

"Roads," said Jack Smith.

"Temples," said Verbushan Patel.

"Ruins," said Neil Phillips.

"Well they didn't build ruins, Neil," Mrs Russell remarked. "They became ruins when they got very old."

"My grandma's a ruin," said Darren Kelly. "She said so."
Some of the children laughed.

"I think she was joking, Darren," Mr Smithers suggested.

"Now, who can tell me what language the
Romans spoke?"

This time there was total silence.

Then, "Please, sir," said a small voice at the back of the
group. It was Spider McDrew.

"Yes, Spider?" Mr Smithers prompted.

Spider smiled. "Baths, sir," he said cheerfully.

Some of the children giggled. "The Romans
spoke baths?" Mr Smithers asked, which made the
children giggle even more. Spider frowned.

"No, sir, they built baths," he said.

"My mum took me to see some. They had hot water that
came out of the ground."

Mr Smithers stared at Spider and shook his head. If anyone looked like they needed a hot bath then it was Spider McDrew. His face was smudged with ink and so were his fingers, and there were streaks of what looked like yellow paint in his sticky-up hair.

"Yes, Spider, the Romans did build baths," Mr Smithers said with a sigh, "but I asked what language they spoke."
"Oh," said Spider.

Mr Smithers told the class that the Romans spoke Latin. Then he told them to listen very carefully to his instructions. He said that the class was to be split into two groups – one would go with him and the other with Mrs Russell. Everyone had to stay in their group while they were in the museum. No one was to wander off on their own.

"Is that clear?" Mr Smithers asked.
"Yes, sir," the class replied.
"Good," said Mr Smithers. Then he split the class into two. Spider was in Mrs Russell's group.

CHAPTER 3

They started their tour by climbing a wide stone staircase that had lion statues on either side. Straight ahead was a white marble statue of a man throwing a discus.

Hannah Stewart put her hand to her mouth.

"Miss, miss, he hasn't got any clothes on," she said.

A couple of the other girls sniggered.

"Don't be silly, now, girls," Mrs Russell said. "It's just a statue."

They carried on climbing. The sign at the
top of the stairs had arrows pointing right
to Greece and Rome and left to Egypt.
That must be where the mummies are,
thought Spider longingly.
"Come along, Spider," Mrs Russell
ordered, as she led her group into the
right-hand room.

Greece and Rome

Egypt

In the gallery there were lots of glass cases with small displays on different things about Roman life – farming, building, art, music, games … Jason Best, Kip Keen and Neil Phillips gawped at a display about gladiators.

Spider preferred the busts of men and women that were in front of the cases. A lot of them looked strange because their noses had broken off. Spider pinched his nose and tried to imagine what it would be like if you couldn't smell anything.

"Whatever are you doing, Spider?" Mrs Russell inquired
with a little wobble of her head.

"Oh, I'm …" Spider began. But at that moment he saw
something in one of the display cases behind Mrs Russell
and his mind wandered. "… a crocodile."

"You're a crocodile?" said Mrs Russell and her head
wobbled even more.

"No, I …" He wanted to explain that he'd just seen a very
interesting statue of a crocodile, but his tongue seemed
to have frozen in his mouth and no words would come.

"Spider McDrew, you are a hopeless case," said Mrs
Russell, and she walked away.

CHAPTER 4

Spider took a closer look at the statue. There was a man on top of the crocodile – or at least his hands were on the crocodile. His body and legs were stretched up in the air. He looked like he was laughing and so did the crocodile. It made Spider want to laugh too. He read the card underneath. It said "An Egyptian acrobat balancing on a crocodile."

There were some other small statues too, and some words that said that Egypt was part of the Roman Empire and that the Romans even worshipped some Egyptian gods, like Isis. Suddenly Spider's mind wandered back to ancient Egypt and mummies. A moment later his feet started to wander too, as he went back through the Roman gallery, past the sign at the top of the staircase and into the room marked "Egypt".

He gazed about in wonder.
The displays were full of
mummies and mummy cases.
The cases were painted in
bright colours and with lots of
little pictures of animals and
birds and hieroglyphic writing.

Many of the mummy cases
were standing up on end.
They were shaped like people
with their arms crossed in
front of them. They were
amazing. So were the
mummies themselves, all
bound up in cloth.

But the exhibits that Spider
loved best of all weren't of
human mummies, but
animals. There was a jackal,
a bird, a fish, and even a
little cat.

Spider's favourite was the cat. It had a friendly, smiling face with lovely greeny-blue eyes.

He was drawing a picture of it when a group of school children came into the gallery. Spider suddenly remembered where he was supposed to be. He said goodbye to the cat and then went off to find the others in his class. But the others weren't in the Roman gallery. Spider walked right through it but there was no sign of Mrs Russell or the children. They must have gone downstairs, Spider thought.

CHAPTER 5

At the bottom of the stairs there was a sign pointing to more Greek and Roman galleries. Spider walked that way. He hadn't gone far, though, when he saw something that made his mind wander completely.

It was another Egyptian room, full of statues. These weren't like the statues in the Roman room – they were huge and extraordinary. Spider had to go in and look. He walked past enormous pillars and massive statues of kings and gods and animals.

Then Spider came to the most amazing thing of all –
a great, green, stone sarcophagus. He climbed up a
step and peered inside. It looked like a gigantic bath,
but this was a real Egyptian mummy's tomb.
What would it be like to be buried inside this?
Spider wondered. An instant later, he had pulled
himself up and over the edge of the sarcophagus.
He lay flat at the bottom with his eyes closed.
He stretched his arms out stiffly alongside his body,
like the mummies he'd seen in the gallery upstairs.

"Spider! Spider McDrew!" Spider opened his eyes to see the red and wobbling face of Mrs Russell staring down at him. "Get out of there at once! Whatever do you think you are doing?" she hissed angrily. Spider's mind slipped back into the present. He flushed as he realised what he had done.

"I'm sorry, Mrs Russell," he said, getting up. "I ... I ..." But it was no good, his tongue had frozen again and he couldn't explain.

CHAPTER 6

Spider was in big trouble. He got a telling off from Mrs Russell and Mr Smithers and a man from the museum. The man was very cross. He said that Spider was lucky not to be banned from the museum for ever. Spider was very sorry.

He was very miserable too. In the coach on the way home he sat at the front on his own, opposite Mr Smithers and Mrs Russell, looking like he might cry.

Mr Smithers looked at the work that the children had done in the museum. Every now and then he would turn around and call out something like, "Well done, Hannah, you worked very hard," or "Darren, there's more to the Romans than fighting, you know!" When he came to the last sheet, he frowned. "Spider," he sighed, "what is this?"

Spider took the sheet and looked at the drawing he'd done. "It's a cat, sir," he said.

"And what does that have to do with Ancient Rome?" his teacher demanded.

Spider gaped at his teacher helplessly. Emma Flowers came to his rescue. "Please, sir. I've got a postcard of that cat," she said. She held it up for Mr Smithers to see. "And on the back, it says it's from the Roman period."

Suddenly Spider's mind was back in place. "Egypt was part of the Roman Empire," he explained. "The Romans worshipped some of their gods."

Mr Smithers nodded. "Well, Spider," he said, "it seems like you did learn something about Ancient Rome after all." He smiled. Spider beamed. Then his grin turned to a puzzled look.

"Sir, were acrobat mummies buried upside down?"
he asked.

Mr Smithers laughed. "Spider McDrew," he declared,
"you really are a hopeless case."

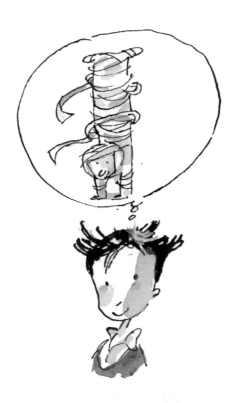

GREECE AND ROME

EGYPT

Ideas for guided reading

Learning objectives: Learning objectives: how dialogue is presented in stories; be aware of different voices using dramatised readings; take account of grammar and punctuation when reading aloud; express views about a story; present events and characters through dialogue

Curriculum links: History: Romans; Ancient Egypt; Art and Design: Investigating patterns

Interest words: Romans, museum, Egyptians, mummies, ancient, gladiator, crocodile, acrobat, Roman Empire, hieroglyphic writing, sarcophagus

Resources: whiteboard, computer

Getting started

This book can be read over two guided reading sessions.

- Read the front and back covers together. Ask the children if they have visited a museum and to share their experiences.
- Look at the pictures on the front cover. *Can the children identify the artefacts? Do they know what they were used for?*
- Share any facts that they know about the Romans or the Egyptians.
- Ask the children, based on their experiences of museum visits, what may happen to Spider at the museum.

Reading and responding

- Model reading pp2-3 of the story to the children using appropriate expression and voices.
- Ask pairs to discuss Spider McDrew's character. *Do they think that he likes school, has many friends?*
- Ask them to read to the end of chapter 1 quietly. Focus their attention on the punctuation to help read the dialogue with expression.